Voices
IN THE PARK

Anthony Browne

DK PUBLISHING, INC.

DK Publishing, Inc.
345 Hudson Street
New York, New York 10014

Visit us on the World Wide Web at http://www.dk.com

Designed by Ian Butterworth

Library of Congress Cataloging-in-Publication Data
Browne. Anthony.
Voices in the park/ written and illustrated
by Anthony Browne.- 1st cd. p. cm.
Summary: Lives briefly intertwine when two youngsters meet in the park.
ISBN 0-7894-2522-X (HC)
978-0-7894-8191-7 (PB)
[1. Gorilla-Fiction. 2. Parks-Fiction. 3. Dogs-Fiction.]
1. Title.
PZ7.B8I984Vo 1998 [E]dc21
97-48730 CIP AC
009-ID046-Dec/2011

Printed in China

First American Paperback Edition. 2001
Published simultaneously in the United Kingdom
by Transworld Publishers Ltd.
15 12 11 10 9

It was time to take Victoria, our pedigree Labrador, and Charles, our son, for a walk.

When we arrived at the park,
I let Victoria off her leash.
Immediately some scruffy
mongrel appeared and started
bothering her. I shooed it off,
but the horrible thing chased
her all over the park.

I ordered it to go away, but it took no notice of me whatsoever. "Sit," I said to Charles. "Here."

I was just planning what we should have to eat
that evening when I saw Charles had
disappeared. Oh dear! Where had he gone?

You get some frightful
types in the park these
days! I called his name for
what seemed like ages.

Then I saw him talking to a very rough-looking child. "Charles, come here. At once!" I said. "And come here please, Victoria."

We walked home in silence.

I needed to get out of the house, so me and Smudge took the dog to the park.

WIFE AND MILLIONS OF KIDS TO SUPPORT.

He loves it there. I wish I had half the energy he's got.

I settled on a bench and looked through the paper for a job. I know it's a waste of time but you've got to have some hope, haven't you?

Then it was time to go. Smudge cheered me up. She chattered happily to me all the way home.

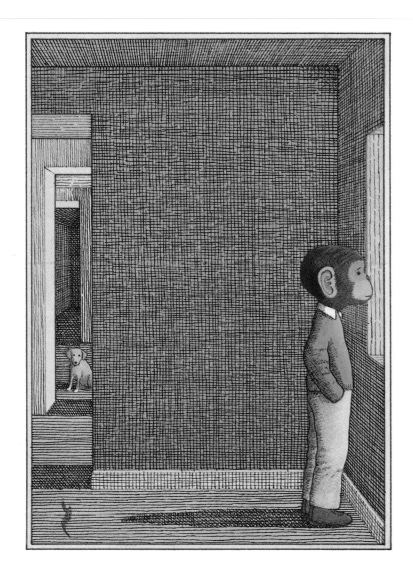

I was at home on my own again.
It's so boring. Then my mother
said that it was time for our walk.

There was a very friendly dog in the park, and
Victoria was having a great time. I wished I was.

"D'you wanna come on the slide?"
a voice asked. It was a girl,
unfortunately, but I went anyway.
She was great on the slide—she
went really fast. I was amazed.

The two dogs raced around like old friends.

The girl took off her
coat and swung on
the climbing bars, so I
did the same.

I'm good at climbing trees,
so I showed her how to do it.
She told me her name was
Smudge—a funny name, I know,
but she's nice. Then my mother
caught us talking together,
and I had to go home.

Maybe Smudge will be there next time?

Dad had been really fed up, so I was happy when he said we could take **Albert** to the park.

Albert's always in such a hurry to be let off his leash. He went straight up to this nice dog and sniffed its backside (he always does that). Of course, the other dog didn't mind, but its owner was really angry, the silly twit.

I got talking to this boy. I thought he was kind of a wimp at first, but he's okay. We played on the seesaw and he didn't say much, but later on he was more friendly.

We both burst out
laughing when we saw
Albert taking a swim.

Then we all played on
the bandstand, and I felt
really, really happy.

Charlie picked a flower
and gave it to me.

Then his mom called
him and he had to go.
He looked sad.

When I got home I put the flower in some
water, and made Dad a nice cup of cocoa.